A NOTE TO PARENTS

When your children are ready to "step into reading," giving them the right books is as crucial as giving them the right food to eat. **Step into Reading Books** present exciting stories and information reinforced with lively, colorful illustrations that make learning to read fun, satisfying, and worthwhile. They are priced so that acquiring an entire library of them is affordable. And they are beginning readers with a difference—they're written on five levels.

Early Step into Reading Books are designed for brand-new readers, with large type and only one or two lines of very simple text per page. **Step 1 Books** feature the same easy-to-read type as the Early Step into Reading Books, but with more words per page. **Step 2 Books** are both longer and slightly more difficult, while **Step 3 Books** introduce readers to paragraphs and fully developed plot lines. **Step 4 Books** offer exciting nonfiction for the increasingly independent reader.

The grade levels assigned to the five steps—preschool through kindergarten for the Early Books, preschool through grade 1 for Step 1, grades 1 through 3 for Step 2, grades 2 through 3 for Step 3, and grades 2 through 4 for Step 4—are intended only as guides. Some children move through all five steps very rapidly; others climb the steps over a period of several years. Either way, these books will help your child "step into reading" in style!

Copyright © 2000 by Berenstain Enterprises, Inc. All rights reserved under International and
Pan-American Copyright Conventions. Published in the United States by Random House, Inc., New York,
and simultaneously in Canada by Random House of Canada Limited, Toronto.

www.randomhouse.com/kids
www.berenstainbears.com

Library of Congress Cataloging-in-Publication Data:
Berenstain, Stan, 1923–
The Berenstain Bears go in and out / by Stan & Jan Berenstain.
p.   cm. — (Early step into reading)
SUMMARY: Going out to eat fast food isn't fast at all when the Berenstain Bears use the revolving door.
ISBN 0-679-89225-7 (trade). — ISBN 0-679-99225-1 (lib. bdg.)
[1. Bears—Fiction. 2. Revolving doors—Fiction. 3. Fast food restaurants—Fiction.]
I. Berenstain, Jan, 1923–   . II. Title.   III. Series.
PZ7.B4483Beoj 2000
[E]—dc21 98-29756

Printed in the United States of America   April 2000   10 9 8 7 6 5 4 3 2 1

Early Step into Reading™

The Berenstain Bears

GO IN AND OUT

Stan & Jan Berenstain

Random House 🏠 New York

Fast food.

Going in.

Around and around.

Coming out.

Going in, again.

Around and around,
again.

Coming out, again.

Going in slowly.

Going out.

Around and around.

Back inside!

Going out, again.

Coming out.

Fast food.